GROOMING HIM
FOR HER

GROOMING HIM
FOR HER

A NOVELLA BY NeCee

HubBooks/Motown Writers

Detroit, Michigan

Buckle up and get ready for a fast ride into NeCee's World of Fantasy, Excitement and Drama. Here, you will have the pleasure of getting to know two dynamic and yet, powerful women, Nikki and Sasha. Pay close attention and learn how Nikki and Sasha spend their time molding brothas—just for you.

Published by
HubBooks/Motown Writers
PO Box 27310, Detroit, MI 48227
http://HubBooks.biz

Book design by
Brenda Lewis
www.ubangigraphics.com • bylewis@ubangigraphics.com

Cover design by
Ivory Wright
http://iwrightdesign.com • ivorywright@gmail.com

ISBN: 0-9774435-2-3

Printed in the United States of America.

Dedication

I dedicate this book to my siblings, Dwight, Gail, Shelia, John, and Sharon. Without their unconditional love, support, and encouragement I wouldn't have been able to complete this journey. I also need to thank my grandmother, Aner Lee Murphy, for her prayers and unwavering confidence in me.

In addition, I have to mention all of the young ladies I've mentored over the years, as well as, anyone who grew up constantly being told that their dreams would never become a reality because of their circumstances, "I'm a living testament that your dreams will come true if only you believe and act on your belief!"

Special Thank You

First, I would like to thank God for always giving me the strength to persevere and overcome life's many obstacles.

Very big thanks to "The Beautiful Ones & Honorary Members" for all of the wonderful and exciting memories we have shared. It is to you, that I must give credit, for my creative and vivid imagination.

For all the people who serve as a mentor in my life. Thank you for helping me realize my potential and always conducting yourself in a way I admire and strive to emulate.

I would also like to take this opportunity to thank everyone who made this project come to life:

- Charleen R. Belue, Friend
- Charisse Smith, Friend
- Cindy Traxler, Editor
- Paris S. Johnson, Hair Care/Stylist (Touch of Elegance)
- Ivory Wright, Photographer/Graphic Artist (I Wright Designs)
- Shay B./Make-Up Artist
- Theresa Green, Model (Sasha)
- Nathaniel D. Frye, Model (Robert)
- Brandy Lewis, Model (Pearl)
- Jennifer Sheffield, Model (Nikki)
- Sterling Cheeks, Model (Brandon)
- Stefanie Wood, Model (Star)
- Aidan Christopher Ivory Wright (Adam)

Everyone that I personally solicited to perform specific tasks (including drive-byes scouting for talent), give input or provide referrals--I thank you and appreciate your time invested in this project.

Last but not least, for those of you who didn't believe in me—I thank you as well. It was you that gave me the courage and determination to complete this project.

In Loving Memory
of Stefanie Belue

Contents

CHAPTER ONE

Disappointment & Self Indulgence

*T*HE RECEPTION WAS COMING to an end; Monique Grier raised her Champagne glass and said, "It gives me great pleasure to recognize such an outstanding attorney this evening. In three short years she has managed to achieve partner status. Her talent has proven to be invaluable to our firm. We are ecstatic to have her on our team. So, on behalf of the firm, please raise your glasses and join me in welcoming our newest, precedent-setting partner, Nikki Ford! Here! Here!"

Nikki stood up, managing a nervous grin, hoping that no one noticed the beads of sweat on her forehead. She wasn't supposed to make partner for another year or two. All the hard work paid off … winning that big products liability case against one of the largest auto manufacturers … for her.

Job offers were flooding in from all over the country. The firm didn't want to lose her, so they immediately offered Nikki a partnership. It was the least they could do, since she was solely responsible for handing over $300 million dollars to the senior partners.

Nikki's walk to the podium made her reminisce about becoming a lawyer. Her dreams were being realized. Those early law school days were tough. Working a full-time job in the City Attorney's office, racing through traffic for four-and-a-half years, the long evenings sitting in class and studying so late that she would fall asleep with her books in her hands had, finally paid off. Proving, once again, that Nikki was a survivor.

Nikki was only six-years old when her oldest brother, Samuel and her parents were killed in a car accident.

Nikki's twenty-one year old sister, Annette raised Nikki and her three brothers. It took Nikki years to realize how much her sister had sacrificed to raise all of them. They were so young Nikki six, Wayne five, Brian ten and Peter twelve.

Nikki was the first member of her family to attend college. When she decided to go on to law school, it was her family's wealth of support and prayers that helped her make it through.

Nikki makes it to the middle of the ballroom and positions herself behind the podium. She adjusts the microphone and speaks with confidence.

"I feel so honored by your recognition. It has always been a dream of mine to become a partner for such a prestigious firm. I remain committed in upholding the reputation of this firm. Thank you for this opportunity." Polite applause filled the room.

Nikki makes her way back to her seat, smiling politely as she shakes hands and accepts congratulations. It feels like an eternity before she arrives back at her seat.

"Congratulations, girl! I'm soooo proud of you. Of course, it was well overdue. Hell, you work damn near seventy or more hours a week for their asses. That's the least they could do for my girl."

Pearl had been by Nikki's side for the past twenty-five years. No matter what the occasion, graduation, public or life event ... Pearl was there, cheering the loudest and holding her hand.

Pearl was the only true friend Nikki had. During the last

semester of high school she will never forget that Tuesday morning, right after second period. Pearl and Nikki shared lockers, they were going to skip third period. It was their senior year and they felt they should do something to celebrate.

Nikki made it to the locker and they were discussing all the fun they were going to have when Nikki felt a pain in her stomach. Pearl could tell something was wrong.

"Are you okay?" Pearl asked, moving closer to Nikki.

Nikki started to respond, but she felt another pain, and then another. She was doubled over, unable to move. Pearl was right by her side.

"I think I should get someone Nik." Pearl started to leave, but Nikki grabbed her arm. Pearl stopped and looked down. Pearl noticed the blood soaking through Nikki's favorite white jeans. Pearl looked nervously around the halls, hoping that no one would come out and find them in the halls. She helped Nikki up and all but carried her to her car.

Pearl droved Nikki to the hospital in silence, she understood what was going on and knew that Nikki didn't want too many questions. They arrived at Baptist Memorial hospital and Pearl checked Nikki in as her older sister.

Pearl sat in the waiting room almost three hours. Nikki came out with a tall, thin, pale-faced doctor. Pearl wasn't sure what to say.

The doctor said, "Make sure she stays off her feet for a few days. She needs some rest." Pearl could only manage a nod. From that day on Pearl has been with Nikki no matter what.

Nikki took her seat next to Pearl and leaned in with a plastic grin on her face. "Girl, you know if they didn't offer me a partner position in the next month or so, my ass was out of here!"

Pearl laughed out loud. "You know you sure have come a

long way since the Pam incident."

Nikki started to laugh. "I haven't thought about her in years."

"I hope not, you might decide to wake me up at 2:00 a.m. again, and girl I don't know that this friendship can take another one of those calls.

Nikki and Pearl laugh so hard they start to cough. Nikki sips on her wine as she recalls that night.

It was 2:00 a.m. when Nikki called Pearl.

"Hello." Pearl managed to push out of her sleepy throat.

Nikki was whispering on the other end. "It's me, are you dressed?"

"I was asleep. What are doing up so late?" Pearl asked after she managed to sit up in the bed.

"I think Raymond is cheating on me."

"He would never do that Nikki, now go back to sleep and call him in the morning." Pearl starts to hang the phone up.

"Wait! I need you to come with me to Pam's house and find out if he's there."

"Pam? Why would Raymond be at Pam's house? He doesn't like her."

"I saw them together earlier acting sort of strange. Would you please come and get me. I need you to drive."

"I don't know Nik. It's late, and Robert is over, what am I'm going to tell him?"

"Please try, I need you, girl."

Pearl couldn't tell Nikki no, so she did what any best friend would do. She threw on a pair of sweat pants, a t-shirt, tennis shoes, and gently kissed Robert on his forehead and said I need to take care of some business. She immediately placed her finger over his mouth and said please don't ask. She made it to Nikki's apartment in no time, to find Nikki pacing backward and forward in the front of her building.

Nikki jumps in the car. "It took you long enough. Do you know where Pam lives?" Pearl nods her head. Pam was a girl who grew up in the same neighborhood as Nikki and Pearl. They wouldn't necessarily classify her as a friend, she was more an associate.

They drive over to Pam's house and see Raymond's car. They go around the block and park across the street and wait.

Nikki explains how Raymond hasn't been calling, and when he does call he's short with her. She goes on about how he comes too fast when they make love. "You know what Auntie Delsie says about men coming too fast it means he's having too much sex elsewhere!"

Pearl didn't know how to respond so she just listened. Nikki keeps on talking, sometimes through her tears, about how much she loves Raymond and how she thought they would be married one day. Pearl tries not to fall asleep, but she can't help herself.

It was about 6:00 a.m. when Raymond comes out of Pam's house.

"Pearl, wake up! He's coming, what should I do?" Before Pearl could comment Nikki was out of the car standing in front of Raymond hitting him and yelling at him. Pearl was right by her side giving Pam the evil eye just hoping that she would jump in so that she could take her out. But, Pam knew that these were some crazy-ass women, so she just stood on her porch watching.

Nikki knew she was blessed to have a friend like Pearl. She had been with her through all of it, even when Nikki went into labor, Brandon was out-of-town on business, Pearl was there to help Nikki push little Isaiah into this world. No matter what went on Nikki knew that Pearl would be with her, she understood that Pearl loved her as her very own sister.

Nikki reached over and grabbed Pearl's hand. "You know you are my girl right?" Pearl nods her head and holds out her hand, making sure her ring is visible.

"And you know I'm married right?" Both of them fall out laughing. Nikki can't help being a bit too sentimental at times … especially with those she loves. When it comes to love, Nikki only knows one way to express it and that's with all of her heart, mind and soul.

Nikki and Pearl continue reminiscing about the old days and enjoy watching everyone watch them. Pearl was the first to notice Matthew.

"Ump ump ump, look who's coming our way! Damnnnn, he's so fine to be a white boy, or should I say European boy? Now you know you ought to give that boy some ass. How long has he been chasing it? And that accent, ooh that accent makes you want to just drop your panties here on the spot!"

"Pearl, calm down! Don't you dare say anything that I'm going to regret." They look at each other and burst out in laughter.

"Allo, loidies. Can someone tell me wot's so funny?"

"Hello, Matthew," Nikki and Pearl said in unison as if they both were caught in a trance of Matthew's tall and lean muscles, naturally tanned skin, dark hair, brown eyes, smelling ooh so good. His Armani suit enhanced his perfect body just enough to make a woman wonder.

"Nikki, congrats agayne, I cawn't think of anyone wot's more deservin'. Please allow me to tike you to dinner so we can celebrate this memorable occoysion, a little more proivately."

Nikki definitely wanted to, but knew she shouldn't. She mumbled under her breath, "Why can't brothas approach me with this same level of confidence?"

"Did you say sommat, Nikki?" Matthew asked.

Nikki flashed a smile and said, "Uhmm, let me think about it."

"Okye, take all the toime you need. Oi got nuttin' but toime. I 'ope you loidies enjoy the rest o' the evening." Matthew looked Nikki straight in the eyes, gently licked his lips, lightly stroked Nikki's left bare arm, and then slowly walks off to speak with other guests.

Pearl hit Nikki in the arm. "You better move on that man before someone else does."

Nikki stared at Matthew for a few more moments. Part of her knew Pearl was right. Matthew was not one to sweat women. Hell, he didn't have to. From time to time, he would let Nikki know he was still interested. He was a single European male, thirty-five years old, no kids, never been married, and had his shit together! He had had his eyes on Nikki the first day she started working at the firm. Nikki learned through the office gossip pool that Matthew was born and raised in East London. His family moved to New York after he completed high school. Matthew attended New York University as an undergraduate and law student. He made partner during his first four years at the firm. He has been a partner for about ten years.

Matthew began his career in the firm's main office in New York. It didn't take long for the firm to recognize his potential. Just six months after he started they sent him to Memphis to groom him for a managing partner position at one of their major city site locations. Matthew is conscientious and secure with himself. He knows what he wants out of life, and coming of age in New York City made Matthew more culturally aware, so he didn't have a problem being attracted to women of color — even in the south.

"Girl, you need to take Matthew up on his offer and give him some poosay!" Pearl's words broke Nikki's stare.

Nikki let out a sigh. "You know I'm taken Pearl. I don't know why you are always trying to set me up with someone and put Brandon down. That's why he never wants to come around, 'cause he knows you don't care for him."

"Don't you put that mess on me. Brandon is a grown man, I'm sorry to say. He knows how to take care of himself. Besides, I wouldn't have to talk about him if he would just treat my girl right. Where is his tired butt anyway?"

Nikki had been hoping that Brandon would show up, because if he didn't, she would never hear the end of it from Pearl. He said that he would try to make this event, and he knew how much it meant to her. Nikki wanted to lie and say that he was working, but Pearl had known her for so long. Hell — the only reason Pearl was asking was to see if Nikki would lie or not.

"You know, I'm not sure where he is, to be quite honest, he said that he would try to make this function. I just don't understand what it is about him avoiding this kind of stuff. It's not like he wouldn't fit in. He's educated and accustomed to associating with people of this status. When I attend some of his work and social functions, he seems very comfortable talking to anyone regardless of who they are. I'm beginning to think it has something to do with me personally."

"It's like this, with Brandon, it's all about him. He needs to be the center of attention. Sure, he wants you to accompany him to his events, because you're his trophy. He enjoys all of the attention he receives from being with you. Haven't you noticed when we all go out how adamant he is about your attire, the way you wear your hair, checking to see if your nails and feet are done? And, I can't leave out the way he displays your credentials every opportunity he gets to his friends, and even to people that he doesn't deal with on a regular basis. Brandon thrives from seeing how envious everyone seems to be of him for having a woman as good as you. Brandon is insecure, easily intimidated, and just can't keep up with you, or handle the attention you receive. Simply put, Brandon has to feel needed. If he did show up here this evening, it would be so obvious that you don't need him."

"Why can't he see me for who I really am? I'm not trying to compete with him or show him up. I need him, but not for material things. I wish he could see that I only want his attention, strength and support. Pearl, I know it's hard for you to understand why I'm still with him, but I see great potential in him."

"I know, Girl. You know he's my boy, but I can't stand to see you hurt. You're such a great catch! Too bad he can't see it."

Nikki flashes a grin. "Remember, you're married!" The two of them start laughing again. Nikki looks down at her watch.

"Oh well, it's getting late, and I'm getting tired of wearing this fake grin, shaking hands and telling everyone thank you for this or that. Let's go."

Right before Nikki turned to leave, she caught Matthew staring at her. He gave her a soft wink, grinned, and nodded his head. At that very moment, a warm sensation ran through Nikki's body and she knew it was time to leave. In the past, it was easy to control the temptation to jump Matthew's bones, but she didn't know what was different about this time. It seemed the more Brandon disappointed her, the more attractive Matthew had become or it may have been the Dom Perignon taking over her body. At any rate, it definitely felt good the way Matthew treated her.

When she got in her car, still smelling Matthew's aroma, she put in her Kenny Lattimore and Chante Moore CD and immediately turn it to track number 5. The music was sounding so good Nikki started to get a little more comfortable. She came to a stop sign, and she slid off her shoes and pantyhose. Nikki started singing with Kenny and Chante, "you are everything I need … yeah sing it Kenny."

She slowly raised her dress and started licking her middle fingers, up and down, up and down. She spread her legs apart, and gently moved her leopard-print thong over enough to insert both fingers, going as far as her fingers would take her. Her clit was moist, but became dripping wet as she moved her fingers in an out, faster and faster. Her body was tingling all over; she had to pull off the road before she hurt somebody. "Good, there's only a few other cars around." Nikki pulled into the Riverside Park Driveway and parked. In the evenings, this was a great place for lovers and even horny individuals like herself to make out. It had a great view of the Mississippi River. She removed the two fingers and inserted them in her mouth and slowly licked every drop of her sweet strawberry scent. Nikki was really turned on by this so she then inserted three fingers, her nipples were hard, and she grew more excited with every touch. Her pussy was so wet, as she moved her fingers in and out, in and out. Her thoughts drifted between Matthew and Brandon. The groans grew louder and louder, she let out a scream, letting go of all her juices.

It took her a moment to collect herself. By the time she calmed down Chante and Kenny were on track number 9, "Off to Wonderland."

"Damnnnn, I need to get home." Nikki drove home feeling calm and satisfied. It was almost midnight when she walked through the door. Brandon had already gone to bed. She looked in on Isaiah, who was dead asleep, snoring even. She didn't want to ruin her high or horniness, so she decided not to make a fuss about Brandon not coming to the reception. She headed straight to the shower, trying to push the thoughts of Matthew out of her mind. It was hard though, she drifted to sleep fantasizing what it would be like to have sex with a white man.

CHAPTER TWO

Raising False Hopes

MOMMY, MOMMY GOOD MORNING! I made you something!" Nikki was always happy to see Isaiah in the morning. Being a mother almost made up for the lack-luster relationship with Brandon.

"Good morning, sweetie! Where are my hugs and kisses?"

Brandon gently stroked the back of Nikki's neck and kissed her on the cheek. Nikki thought, "It's funny how Brandon can show his attention and support for her through Isaiah." Nikki turned on the light, and sat up in bed. She waited as Isaiah and Brandon presented their recognition gift to her.

Tears welled up in Nikki's eyes as she read the hand-made card from Isaiah. She took a deep breath as she fought back her tears.

"Son, it's beautiful! Did you do this all by yourself?" The blue and gray letters spelled out:

Congratulations to my Mommy, A Partner!
I'm so proud of you. Love You Much!
Isaiah

Isaiah had even drawn a picture of a lady with a briefcase symbolizing his mom. Nikki looked at her son and continued to fight back the tears. She was able to fight them off until Isaiah handed her a single yellow rose.

Yellow roses were her favorite flower, and it was the first gift Brandon had ever given her. For some reason it felt so long ago.

"No, Daddy helped me. I'm really proud of you mommy."

"Well, thank you Isaiah. I feel so honored that you would make me such a beautiful card and give me such pretty flower. Where did you get so much money?"

"I saved it from my birthday. I only had five dollars, so Daddy had to give me two more for the flower, but I promised to pay him back."

Nikki kissed Isaiah on the forehead. "Thank you again. You need to get ready for school if you want to have time to eat some pancakes, you know you have that field trip to the petting zoo today, so remember to dress casual … no uniform today!"

Isaiah ran towards his room yelling, "pancakes, pancakes, I get to eat some pancakes and wear my favorite jogging suit!"

Nikki watched him in awe at how tall and handsome he was getting. He looked older than his five years. It seemed like yesterday that she had him, only three months after graduating from law school.

She thought things with her and Brandon would be much better after Isaiah was born.

They had been together for nearly three years before Isaiah was born. She would never admit it to anyone, but she intentionally forgot to take her birth control pills a few weeks right before she got pregnant with Isaiah.

Nikki was in the kitchen making the pancakes she had promised Isaiah. When she heard Kirk Franklin and The Family on the radio, Nikki hurried and turned up the radio dial so that she could get her praise on with Kirk. This was one of Nikki's morning rituals. Before she starts each day, she has to give thanks to God for her many blessings and to give Him the praise He so much deserves.

Brandon walks up behind her and grabs her around the waist. It felt good for him to touch her in such a relaxed way. It had been too long since he held her. Brandon was dark, stood at least 6'2" with very broad shoulders. He definitely had that NBA athletic-built going on.

Brandon kissed her on the neck. "Good morning, I hope things went well for you last night."

"Yes, everything went well. However, I really missed you." He pulled away and the cold man she had come to know so well returned.

Brandon had already rehearsed what he was going to say to Nikki. He knew she would have something to say about him not being there. He wanted to be there for her, but he just wasn't in the mood to deal with all those rich, arrogant, fake ass people. He refused to attend another "why is she still with him?" event.

When Nikki won her first big case, the firm gave a reception in her honor. The first question everyone asked Brandon was "what do you do for a living?" When he responded that he was a team leader at the United Package Service, the conversation didn't seem stimulating enough to continue.

"I'm so sorry I couldn't be there last night. We've been having some theft problems occurring on the second shift and I had to stick around to investigate. Besides, I haven't been to my apartment in over a week and I needed to check on it. I wasn't trying to miss your big night, but it's better that I don't come than to come late, right?" He grabbed hold of her again and pulled her close to him. Nikki could never resist his bright smile and gentle eyes. "I know how important making partner is to you. Let's plan to go out next week to celebrate." Brandon kissed her so deeply that she forgot about the pancakes she had been cooking for Isaiah. It took the fire alarm going off to break the trance he had put her in.

"Here, I have a little something for you to show how much I love you?" Nikki really did feel that Brandon loved her. He just had a funny way of showing it. But Nikki is such a sucker for romance. She opened the card and in his handwriting it read:

There is no one like you. I thank God each day for sending you to me. Can't wait until we become a family and you, my wife.

Love, Brandon

The card accompanied a half dozen of red roses. That was one of the things she loved most about Brandon — genuine and simple. She hugged him for a very long time, letting him know without words that everything was okay.

"Good morning boo, what's up? I hope it's what I think it is …"

Pearl started to move her hands under the silk sheets searching for Robert's second head, which wasn't hard to find. Robert pushed her hand away. He immediately noticed the look of disappointment in her face. He grabbed hold of her hand and leaned in to kiss her on the cheek.

"I love you, but you know I don't like to do it in the morning, especially when I have to go to work in a couple of hours. I'll be exhausted for the rest of the day. I really need to be alert today."

Robert worked for the Memphis International Airport in the IT/Air Traffic Control Department. He enjoyed working, working and hunting. Robert's smooth, chocolate skin and well-groomed beard made Pearl shiver with excitement every time she laid her eyes on him. It didn't hurt that he was six-feet-five-inches tall, lean, and muscular with a size 14 shoe either. Pearl has been hooked on the man since the day she met him.

Even though Robert was well endowed, having sex any time of the day in every which way is not one of his top priorities. His idea of having sex consisted of one position, after sunset, about once or twice a week. Pearl hadn't had that much experience in the sex department. It wasn't that Pearl some kind of freak, she had only slept with two other men before Robert. But at least she had experienced the pleasure of giving, and receiving, a lube job and performing sexual acts in the most inconspicuous places.

Pearl was careful not show all of her frustration, her mother had taught her better than that. But, she was growing impatient with Robert. He hadn't even noticed the new skimpy lingerie she had on. "You have to go into work early again? You promised that we could have sex one morning this week. I was hoping it was going to be today! I need you, I want you."

Robert leaned in and kissed her on the lips. "I'm sorry baby, but I have to get to work. I know I made you a promise, and it will happen, just not this morning. By the way I love the new teddy, it's my favorite color too, make sure you wear again, okay?" Pearl spent most of her spare time trying to look and dress sexy for her man. She has that dark brown skin tone with the most amazing brown eyes. She's small frame but has a very attractive shape that would catch most guys' attention.

Pearl had to push back her smile. She knew she had a good man. "Okay, but I'm not letting you off the hook."

Robert was relieved. He quickly got moving, jumped in the shower, and was off to work. Sometimes he felt Pearl, women in general, were obsessed with sex. He felt that way because women came on to him all the time, especially at work. He didn't see himself as handsome. He didn't even dress sexy. He wondered what it was about him that made women go wild for him.

"Good afternoon, Robert. How are you?"

"Hello, Sasha. I'm doing well. Robert said with a smile." He had been noticing Sasha for some time, but made a point not to let it show. He didn't want anyone accusing him of sexual harassment or anything.

Sasha Benay was a TransAmerican Airlines director in customer service. Of all the women that had come on to him, Sasha was the only one he often thought about sinning with. Sasha was a fine, five-foot, eight inches, 145 pounds, smooth chocolate skin, long beautiful hair that she wears in braids most of the time, perfect nails and teeth, and a body women wish they had, and men wish they could spank. She even looked great in her TransAmerican uniform. She would flirt with Robert from time to time, but it was done very tastefully and discretely. Today felt different for Robert, he decided to flirt back just for the fun of it.

"How about coffee later?" Sasha asked.

Sasha was expecting him to respond with his usual, "maybe." She almost lost her cool when he accepted. She had been trying for months to get him to a least look at her like he wanted her. He was a challenge now, someone that she just wanted to see if she could be with.

Sasha was thinking to herself, "this brotha doesn't know who he's messing with." Sasha treated men like boy toys. She enjoyed her single life to the fullest. With her flight benefits, she had men in different states and countries. She often reflected on something her granny used to tell her about men, *"Honey, let every state furnish their own man."* Lord, knows her granny didn't mean for her to have a man in every state or country. Sasha decided to expand her granny's scope to cover states and countries and just stick with granny's literal meeting. Sasha chuckled at the thought.

It was around 3:00 p.m., and Robert started walking towards Starbucks. Sasha was also walking towards Starbucks, but in the opposite direction. As he walked down the corridor, Sasha visualized what it was going to be like having sex with his tall lanky self.

She pictured herself pinned to the back of her office door, straddling him, arms flying in the air as if she was at church feeling the holy spirit, then holding his face gently but firm right between her 36D breasts ….

"Sasha, Sasha, where would you like to sit?" Robert's sexy voice broke her soon-to-be wet dream. Sasha was embarrassed.

"Oh, oh, oh, I'm sorry, I don't know where my mind was, how about over here in the corner. Can you please order me a regular coffee with two raw sugars?"

As Robert walked over to the table, Sasha was pleading to "Jane" to calm the hell down. But, nooooo there she goes, getting all moist and bothered. Sasha tried harder to shake those visuals of Robert out of her head. This was a bad time for Sasha. She'd been off the rag for two days and was hornier than ever.

"So, Robert, tell me about yourself." Robert appeared to be extremely nervous. Every time Sasha opened her mouth, he looked to his left then to his right before responding. You would think they had just committed the crime of adultery and he was about to be stoned by Jesus, himself. Sasha could tell right off that this was probably his first thought about being naughty. Sasha thought to herself, "this brotha doesn't have a clue, doesn't he know he's messing with fire!"

"Well, I have been married for seven years, and working for the Airport for about 14 years."

"Do you have children?"

"No, none yet, one day we will though." Robert tried to push the nervousness out of him voice, but he couldn't stop thinking about Pearl. He didn't want to hurt her, but there was something about Sasha from the way she licked her lips to the way she walked. She was just too sexy.

"Is that it, surely your life is more exciting than that. How do you like to be entertained?"

"I enjoy reading mysteries and hunting."

"You see, we have something in common. I enjoy reading as well. When I'm not traveling, my normal routine on a Sunday is going to church, brunch, and Starbucks for coffee and reading. You ought to join me sometime, and we can read together."

Robert knew that he would do things with Sasha he shouldn't be doing if he met her for coffee, tea, or hot chocolate. The meeting would just be the appetizer to a meal he couldn't wait to sink his teeth in.

"I don't know if we should ..."

Sasha stopped Robert by putting her finger over his mouth. "You don't have to worry about me I'm a big girl. I'm not looking to break you and your wife up. I only want to have a little fun. Don't you think we could have fun?" Sasha was just too breathtaking. Her hands were even softer than he imagined.

Robert let a smile go, trying to push back images of him and Sasha in bed with her riding him. "I just might take you up on your offer." He didn't understand why she was so interested in him. In his world, no woman would or could be satisfied being the "other" woman. Not only had she sparked his curiosity, he couldn't wait to get a taste of her body.

"So, tell me, what do you like to hunt?"

"Uhmmm, deer, wild turkey, duck, rabbit, … you name it, I will or am willing to hunt it."

"Wow, how exciting! I often wondered what enjoyment one gets out of hiding, lying, and waiting for the right opportunity to catch its prey."

"It's more than just mere excitement. It's more like a release of tension, relaxation and dominance … all emotions working together, simultaneously. Hunting is more than just a sport to me, it teaches you things that are not easily learned in life. For instance, let's take discipline and patience. There are many guidelines when it comes to hunting. Such as, hunting deer, you can only do so during daylight hours. You have to start early and be extremely organized because you don't have time to loose. I can recall many times hanging in a tree for hours in the cold, rain, high winds, just for the hunt … not even thinking twice about giving up. I owe much of my life successes to this game. I apply those same principles to my personal life and career."

"Quite the sportsman, you are. I didn't think hunting was that serious. You have definitely peaked my interest. I could use a little patience and discipline in my life. Perhaps, you could teach me a thing a two."

"Really? So, you're telling me that you would be willing to dress up in camouflage and bright orange gear, cap, vest, boots and use a 30 30 rifle?"

"Yes."

"Waking up around 5:30 in the morning, getting into position around 6:45, and waiting in the same position for 3–6 hours at a time …"

"Yes."

"Staying overnight at a camp site, sleeping in a tent, in the month of November in the countryside of Oakland, Tennessee?"

"Yes, no problem."

"You are something else!"

"Hey, when you're ready to give me lessons, here's my number, call me."

Chapter Three

Reality Check

*H*ELLO, HELLO."

Their voices rang out in unison as they picked up the phone.

"I got it Adam, you can hang up."

"Okay Mom."

"Hey, Girlee. You're going to church this morning?" The South is known for its big churches and everybody who was somebody usually attended Christian Fellowship Church — downtown Memphis. Membership was well over 10,000. Sasha and Star have been members for about seven years, and this was one of the things they did together as a way to bond.

"Yes, you want me to stop by and pick you up?"

"Yes please."

"Okay, Adam and I will be there in the next hour or so."

It's been almost five years since Star's husband, Marcus, was killed by accident while cleaning his hunting gun. However, the street committee says that he committed suicide because of the pressures of a new marriage, then a year later having a child, and shortly after Adam was born, Marcus was laid off from his six-figure income job due to restructuring at International Business Inc.

It took a couple of years after Marcus's death, for Star to

overcome some serious emotional trauma. She had trouble sleeping and eating. She didn't want to come out of the house, and poor Adam got no attention at all. Star didn't mean to ignore her son, but he looked so much like his father that she couldn't bear to see him.

She has bounced back, but has been slow to establish a new relationship. Her main focus had been on Adam. However, she really felt that since Adam was turning six this year, he needed a male figure in his life. She decided to look into some of the ministries at church that might be able to help.

"Adam, are you almost ready?

"Yes ma'am!" Adam yelled back to his mother.

"Then look in the pantry and get you a pop tart and I think there's juice in the fridge. We don't have a lot of time, we have to stop and pick up your Tee Tee Sasha."

"Okay, I'll hurry mom!"

Adam was well-mannered and very mature for his age. He was only a year old when his father passed away. His mom would tell him that he was the man of the house. He tried to act like one too. He would bring his mom the only breakfast he knew how to cook, a pop-tart and apple juice, in bed. He would hold her hand when he would see her crying, promising her that she would feel better if she took a nap. Adam really tried to take care of his mother, and Star had come to rely on him more than she should.

"What's up with you? Star asked as Sasha put on her seat belt.

Sasha started to open her mouth, but Star stopped her. "Wait a minute; let me turn up the music so that Adam is not all up in our business." Star knew how wide open Sasha could be. Sasha tended to say whatever was on her mind.

"Girl, let me tell you. You know that nerdy, fine, Mandingo looking guy I've been fishing at work. Well, I've caught him. We had coffee yesterday and now I'm waiting to reel him in. Sasha's throaty laugh confirmed that she was deep in her games.

It's funny how Sasha could tell in a matter of minutes how well a man was going to perform in bed. She claimed a man's confidence, hand shake, and eyes told it all. She definitely had a great track record for finding the right man to satisfy her the way a woman should be satisfied. On the other hand, it only took her a matter of seconds to sense when a man ain't got shit going on between his legs.

She would ask one question, "How important is sex to you in a relationship?" An insecure man usually starts by saying, "sex isn't everything," or "sex is overrated," or "too much emphasis is placed on sex."

A secure, well-endowed man would answer in a confident way, "I think sex is very important, even more important is pleasing my woman, doing whatever, whenever, however." And then, if a secure man added that he worked out, didn't drink or do drugs, and took ginseng on the regular, a woman was in for the time of her life, according to Sasha.

"Are you ever going to settle down?"

"Why should I? I'm having too much fun. Besides, I'm a beautiful, black, independent, don't-need-a-man-to-take-care-of-me-financially, woman. Girl, men have juggled several women around at one time for years and society has accepted their behavior just fine. It's my turn now. And, I do believe I've hit the jackpot this time. I'm going to teach Robert to take me places he's never been before!" Star and Sasha laughed together.

"Girl, you are too much! We need to get our minds on the Lord now, I just saw Sister Aner staring at us and you know how nosey she is."

Star and Sasha have been true friends. They have known

each other since they were five-years old. They had learned to accept each other for who they were, not wasting precious time trying to change each other, and still managed to maintain a great friendship. They knew everything there was to know about each other and never judged one another for the decisions they made, bad or good, and just accepted each other for who they were.

~·~

"Baby, sit up straight. After the offering, you can go to children's church."

"Mommy, do I have to? Why can't I stay here with you?"

"Sweetheart, Children's Church has been designed especially for you by the Lord. You don't want to disappoint the Lord and not attend, do you?"

"No."

"Well then, I'll pick you up right after church. Now give me a kiss, and you better listen closely because you know I'm going to quiz you later when we get home."

"Okay, Mommy."

As the visiting minister approached the podium, the music to Mary J's "Real Love" started playing

"Real love, I'm searching for a real love, someone that'll set my heart free … I'm searching for a real love and don't know where to go"

"Are you searching for that perfect, true and unconditional love? Let me see a show of hands of those of us who are searching for that perfect, true and unconditional love." The power of her words made everyone sit up and pay attention. Everyone knew right away that she was a real preacher, not just another woman riding the suite jacket of her husband.

Of course Nikki didn't raise her hand, because in her

mind, she has found the perfect love.

The minister goes on in her throaty voice, "Webster's defines perfect as complete or correct in every way, true as faithful to another, genuine sincere and unconditional as absolute, without qualifying conditions and last love."

"Now, we will discuss what Webster's has to tell us about love. It reads, 'it is a powerful emotion felt for another person manifesting itself in deep affection'."

Okay, now we got to check and see what the Lord tells us about perfect, true and unconditional love. Turn with me to 1 John 4:18. It reads:

> *'There is no fear in love. But perfect love drives out fear, because fear has to do with punishment. The one who fears is not made perfect in love.'*

"Now turn to 1 Corinthians 13:5, it tells us:"

> *'Love is not rude, it is not self-seeking, it is not easily angered, it keeps no record of wrongs.'*

" So, according to the Bible and Webster's to experience this perfect, true and unconditional love, one must be correct in every way, faithful, accept all faults of another, fearless, kind, and with high integrity. Now, let me see again a show of hands of those of us who are searching for that perfect, true and unconditional love." This time the hands doubled, including Nikki's. Nikki pushed away the tears she felt welling up in her eyes, she knew that she didn't have a perfect love. Perfect love has to be shared by both people.

The minister was on fire, she continued on and asked the congregation, "What is keeping you from experiencing this type love? Men, is it a successful, independent woman scaring you away from commitment? Ladies are you that selfish and conniving that you're only concerned about your needs, and don't care about how many families you have broken up due to your promiscuous behavior?" Sasha nudged Star with her elbow and whispered, 'Ouch.' "Okay, husbands and wives, your spouse messed up and you haven't been speaking or sleeping in the same bed for over a week ... when are you going to learn to let it go?! Let it burn. Let it burn. Let it burn." Real love doesn't keep records of wrong!"

The congregation was roaring, "Amen, Amen," "Sister preach that word!" "Say it!"

"I'm here to tell you that there is hope, but it's going to require some work from you. I know you're sitting there thinking, 'how can I experience this type love?'... keep in mind that love is a verb, meaning love must be practiced or performed — you must show action and do it consistently! True love is not PRIVATE or shouldn't be kept a secret. True love is shown to the world without a care to those who do not approve. True love is not meant to be kept in a bottle or proven behind closed doors. Turn to your neighbor and say, Talk is cheap, show me you love me!"

"The Lord shows us daily His love for us. He gave us His most precious gift, His son. He even loved us when we turned our backs on Him. Oooohhh, you remember, when you promised Him if He would bless you with that job, you would bless Him financially and instead we purchased a convertible Jag, Or the time when He helped you get out of jail, you said that you would live for him! Instead, as soon as you got out of jail, the church was the last place on your mind. Oh yes, let's not forget when you had your $50,000 wedding, in his house I must remind you, and you haven't seen the inside of a church since. And worst of all you stayed on your knees praying for a healthy child, you got one and you raise this child up not knowing the Lord. All of these blessings and what do you do, you go back to the same old lifestyle — God, second. Love is not about compromising, true love is unconditional, God wants you to love Him, just because."

The minister starts to rock back and forth, holding her arms tight around herself. Tears are running down her cheeks, but she is not sad. The congregation calms down and waits for her words to come. She opens her eyes and smiles.

"I'm almost done. Please be patient with me. Turn with me to 1 John 3:18, can someone read this verse for me?"

Sister Aner is always the first to speak when asked to read a verse. She recites, "Dear children, let us not love with words or tongue but with actions and in truth."

The ministers repeats, "... let us not love with words or tongue but with actions and in truth. This confirms that love must be demonstrated."

"I see some people sitting there still confused about how to practice this type of love. First, we must show our love for God by accepting his son, Jesus as our Lord and Savior, and believing in our hearts that Jesus died on the cross so that we may have eternal life. It's that simple. Then we must repent our fears, unfaithfulness, destruction of others, and our unforgiving hearts. I know that this is hard to try on a person, that's why we first must try this new love on God, and he'll provide us with the strength that is needed to face our fears, our acts of infidelity, and cruel spirits head on. As we continue to show our love for Him, He will teach us how to love others and recognize the sincerity in others as they show their love for you. I'm almost done. This sermon cannot be complete if I didn't share with you the consequences of not showing love in this fashion, which could be brutal. Turn with me for the last time to 1 John 4:19, let us read this together, I want you all to know how serious this is.

'For anyone who does not love his brother, whom he has seen, cannot love God, whom he has not seen. Whoever loves God must also love his brother.'

"Now, everyone stand, and those of you who love God

and want to live for him, come, show God you love him, by stepping out of your seat and joining me in the front of the church."

Nikki thought to herself, *Wow, is this really how two people are supposed to love one another? Is this how people are supposed to love, period? Is it even possible?*

Nikki could feel her cell phone vibrating. It was the third time it rang. She wondered, 'who it could be calling?' She reached into her purse and glanced at her cell phone. It was Brandon calling her. He knew she was at church. Good thing church had ended. She went out into the vestibule and returned Brandon's call. All she could hear was trembling in his voice, she asked if he was at home, and said that she would be right there.

She decided that since she didn't know what was going on with Brandon, she would drop Isaiah off at her grandmother's. She used her key to let herself into Brandon's apartment. He was sitting in his living room, blinds closed; all the lights in the apartment were off. She approached him very slowly, not knowing what to think. She asked, "What's wrong, honey?"

"He's gone, and I didn't get a chance to say goodbye."

"Who's gone, honey?"

"My dad and I had an argument, and he put his hand over his chest, I realized he was having a heart attack. Momma called 911, but he died in my arms. Nik, I didn't get a chance to make it right between us. I didn't get a chance to tell him I really did respect and love him. It's too late, Nik, it's too late. Nik, it's my fault. I pushed him over the edge this time … I'm sorry, I'm sorry."

Brandon and his father had been estranged for many years. Brandon's father lived an extraordinary life. He started off as a lobbyist for a major automotive company. He served as a city councilman for twelve years, mayor for eight years and recently had appointed to the Board of Directors for General Motor Company in Nashville. Brandon was an only child. His father had high, but sometimes unrealistic, expectations for Brandon's life. Brandon never seemed to measure up to his father's standards, so he became very distant with both his parents. Brandon rarely talked about their relationship.

Deep in Brandon's heart he loved his parents, but he didn't know how to show them. It wasn't totally Brandon's fault. Love is taught and Brandon's parents were much too busy to do that. With all the political events, dinners, parties, and the demands of the public, many family principles were often spoken about, but very little values were practiced in the Adams' household. What Brandon really wanted was to ask his father to forgive him ... forgive him for not pleasing him, forgive him for always being rebellious, forgive him for being just plain old stubborn. Brandon fantasized about how he wished he and his father could have watched a football game together, drank a beer while attending a college basketball game, shared intimate chats about women and relationships, or played a game of pool. For years, Brandon kept on putting off talking with his father. He never attempted to make amends. Now, it was too late, his father was gone.

Nikki sat right beside Brandon and held his head between her breast and whispers, "Sweetie, I can't imagine what you're going through, but I do know you will get through this. You must trust that your father is in a better place."

"But, Nik, what am I going to do, what can I say to my mother, she must hate me."

"Your mom does not hate you. Your mom really needs you right now. If you want to show your father how much you love him, you need to be strong and be there for your mom, while she's here ... don't shut her out."

Brandon can't control his tears; Nikki gently places both

her hands on each side of Brandon's face and softly kisses his cheeks.

"Baby, I love you, and I'm going to see you through this."

"Nik, I don't know what I would do without you in my life."

Chapter Four

Piece of Cake

ROBERT COULDN'T SEEM TO get Sasha off his mind. Four days had gone by since they last spoke. He was hoping by now that they would accidentally run into each other at work. He dare not call her. But his curiosity was getting the best of him. Finally, after not being able to think of anything else except the smell of her perfume and her perfect smile, Robert decided after work he would take the long route when exiting the airport.

There she was … talking with some customers. Robert couldn't help but to stop and stare at her. Sasha's smile and poise were mesmerizing. Sasha glanced to her left just enough to notice his presence. She knew what he had come for so she made it worth his effort. First, she took her left hand and tucked a portion of her hair neatly behind her left ear. As she released her fingers, she gently massaged the left side of her neck and turned her back to him. As the customers started walking off Sasha removed her jacket, placed it on the ticket counter and slowly took both hands and rested them on each side of her curvy and voluptuous hips and thighs. Robert stood there. He couldn't move. Sasha turned around, smiled and started walking his way.

"Robert, how have you been? Haven't seen you around, lately."

Robert dabbed at the beads of sweat on his forehead. "I'm fine. I was on my way out and I wanted to say hello, but I noticed that you were busy. I didn't want to disturb you while you were working."

"I was just about to meet my girlfriend at Isaac Hayes for dinner. Would you like to join us?"

"No, but thank you for the offer."

"You should call me, so we could hook up for coffee, reading, or whatever." Sasha's grin communicated more than coffee and reading.

"Okay, I will. I will call you tomorrow around 2:00 to see what would be a good time for you. I just purchased "The Testament" by John Grisham. I've been trying to find some time to get started."

Sasha thought to herself, damn, this boy really hasn't done this before. What's up with this calling at 2:00? This is going to be too easy!

"I'll look forward to your call, at 2:00." Sasha couldn't help but to giggle.

Star was getting irritated that Sasha wasn't answering her phone. "She's probably flirting with some man knowing her. I just hope it's not that Mandingo man she had her eye on last week … if so, I know I've been stood up. I guess I'll try one last time and if she doesn't answer I'm going home." The phone rings 3 times and Star paces back in forth hoping no one notices her talking to herself.

On the sixth ring Sasha picks up, Star doesn't let her say a word. "Girl, where are you? I've been waiting for 20 minutes. You did say Isaac Hayes? Right?"

"Awe Girl, I'll be right there. It's not like you have somewhere else to go. I'm around the corner. Try to get our regular seating at the bar. Is Moses bartending tonight?"

"Yes, he is."

"Great! That means all drinks are on the house!"

Ever since Marcus passed away, Sasha had made every effort to force Star to have dinner with her at least twice a week — after church and one day during the week. Isaac Hayes was one of their favorite spots, especially on Thursdays. On Thursdays, Fresh Ideas hosts an after work jazz extravaganza. Of course, Sasha was "chummy chummy" with the owner of Fresh Ideas, Michael Powell. Mike always went out of his way to make sure Sasha was well taken care of. The moment she enters the door, it was VIP service. No waiting in line, no cover charge — no hassles. Sasha and Star enjoy sitting at the bar, sipping on their favorite kind of Merlot or on Thursdays, it's Champagne, listening to the jazzy beats of Miles Davis and people watching. It was one of the hottest spots in downtown, Memphis.

"I'm heeere. Girl, sorry I'm late. I got a little held up at work. You remember Mr. Nerdy, IT guy ..." and Sasha whispered, "with the extremely big dick."

"Have you gotten with him already!?"

"No, not yet."

"Girl, I still can't figure out this radar you have detecting big dicks. But, I must admit, it works. I remember the guys we would pick up at bars, before I got married of course. You were right about their potential big, or in some cases, little bedroom performances!" Sasha and Star gave each other high fives and started giggling.

"Hello, Ladies. Mike has given me strict orders to take very good care of you this evening. So, what would you like?"

"Besides you?"

Moses always blushed at Sasha's flirtatious comments. Moses was 6'5, about 265 pounds, muscular build, smooth dark brown skin, baldheaded with a well-manicured beard, and very mild-mAnered. You would never see Moses flirt with too many women. He was happily married and well-tamed.

"Well, since I can't sip on you, we'll share a bottle of Champagne. Your very best bottle of Dom Perignon, please."

"Your wish is my command. Here are some menus and I shall return."

Mike spots Sasha and Star at the bar and headed their way. "I was hoping to see you and Star this evening. You ladies are looking scrumptious tonight ... and you, Sasha, you look good enough to eat."

"Okay, Mike, don't play ..."

Aaaha, Champagne this evening, I see Moses is really taking care of my girls."

"Yes he isss" Sasha said in an extremely sexy and seductive voice.

Both ladies said at the same time, "Thank you, Mike!" Sasha leans over to give Mike a kiss.

"Anything for the most beautiful ladies in the house." Mike takes his right hand and places it midway on Sasha's back, and starts to rub slowly. Mike whispers in Sasha's ear, "Be sure to save me a dance."

Sasha gestures as if she was going to whisper something into Mike's ear, but she sticks out her tongue and gently slides it around his earlobe and kisses him on the jaw."

"Ewee Wee girl, you better stop before you start something you can't finish."

A light-skinned, not that attractive woman walked over to the bar and said to Mike, "you've been avoiding me all evening ... is there a reason?" Mike replied, "no, I've just been chatting with my guests."

Mike turns to Sasha and Star and says, "Excuse me ladies. Let me know if you need anything. And ladies, please don't hurt the brothas too bad tonight."

Sasha and Star starts to giggle.

CHAPTER FIVE

Forgive, Forget & Seal the Deal

NIKKI PACES AS SHE listens to Brandon's phone ring. Just as she is about to hang up she hears him on the other end. "We need to talk. Can I come over?"

"Well, I was just about to meet Ty at the Community Center. Can it wait?"

"No, it can't wait. I'm on my way over." Nikki hangs up and leaves.

Nikki's in her car, talking to herself. "I can't believe the nerve of him. Can it wait? How dare him! I have been there all of this time, waiting for him to want me. Waiting for him to tell me he needs me. I try to understand, but he doesn't even try." Tears start to run down Nikki's cheeks. She slaps them away. "I refuse to cry another day behind this man!"

Nikki pulled into the parking lot of Brandon's building and quickly moved toward the door. She needed some answers; it had been over a month since Brandon's father passed away. Brandon hasn't even bothered to visit, the last time her or Isaiah seen him was at the funeral. She had left message after message, but Brandon never bothered to call her back. She decided, after her fifth glass of wine the night before, and a week off of work, that she needed to know if they would ever be a family. She had already invested too much time in this joint venture.

She decided to use her key to let herself in Brandon's apartment since he knew she was on her way over. Brandon was sitting in the living room watching football; the New York Giants were playing the Tennessee Titans.

Nikki walks over and stands in front of the TV. "Hello."

"Hey, what's up? Could you move over a bit, I can't see the game?"

Nikki crossed her arms in front of her. "I need some answers Brandon. I need to know what's going on with you, with us. You don't bother to call me or check on your son."

Brandon sat back on the couch and stared at Nikki for a moment before he spoke.

"You know I wish I could understand you better. I wish I could be all that you want and need, but that doesn't seem possible. You know how hard my father's death has been on my mother. Hell, you were the one that suggested I spend more time with her, and now you are crying about me not being around. Believe it or not Nikki, this isn't about you."

Nikki wasn't sure what she should do. Brandon always had a way of making her feel bad about complaining. Nikki lowered her arms and sat down next to Brandon.

"Look I don't want to start a fight. I just want to understand why you don't include us in your life. We want to help. Isaiah was even asking about you and his Grandmother. I never know what to say. I thought all of us would help each other and your mom get through this. I didn't think you would exclude us from this critical time in life. How can we ever make a marriage work if we don't talk to each other? You need to talk to me!"

Brandon turns towards Nikki and touches her on the cheek. "Okay, you want me to talk, I'll talk. For starters, I'm still trying to get over my father's death. I just found out a couple of days ago that my company is going through a bankruptcy, and my job has been eliminated. My apartment lease will be up in 30 days, and I'm not sure if I should renew it — since I'm going to be out of a job in two months. I can't stand the thought of you taking care of us. I don't want to live off of you or any other woman. It's really bothering me and it doesn't help when you put pressure on me to marry you."

Nikki slumped back on the couch forcing herself not to cry. "I didn't know. You know I'm here for you."

"Nikki, I don't want you to handle me or make all this better. I just need you to give me some space."

"What does that mean? I just want to be here to help you. We have to take care of each other. If the shoe was on the other foot, you would take care of me. Just let me help." Nikki moved closer to Brandon and reached for his hand, but he moved away.

They sat silent, for what seemed like hours, but were only a few minutes. Nikki got up from the couch and made her way to the door. She wasn't sure what had happened. Her thoughts raced and her spirit was even dimmer than it was when she arrived. Just before she opened the door her defeated words carried faintly through the room. "Baby, it's going to be all right. I'll be here for you — when you're ready. Just call me."

Nikki opened the door and started to leave, but Brandon stopped her. "Stay with me." Nikki turned around; her body was tingling all over. Her nipples got hard when he stared at her. It reminded her of the first night they made love.

"I love you so much. Don't shut me out." Brandon didn't say a word.

Brandon picked Nikki up, pulled her legs around him, pushing her up against the door. The kisses were deep, making Nikki wetter than she had been in years. Nikki pulled off Brandon's shirt, anxious to feel him inside her, while he moved his hands between her legs. Her body was shaking, he was breathing so heavy. The fire was back. Nikki unbuckled his belt and unzipped his pants with one hand. He pulled his pants and boxers down, pinned Nikki up against the door, lifted her skirt, moved her thong to the side, and entered her as deep as he could. Nikki moaned loud as he moved up and down, up and down, over and over, refusing to stop until she let out her familiar screams of ecstasy.

~~

Pearl is up cooking breakfast when Robert wanders into the kitchen. "Good Morning darling." He leans in and kisses Pearl on the cheek.

"Good Morning."

"What do you want for breakfast?"

"I'll just have coffee."

"You need more than coffee. What time is your game this morning?"

"It's at seven o'clock."

"Seven a.m. on a Saturday morning. You have to know I love you."

"Yes, yes I do." Robert poured Pearl some coffee and sat down across from her. "You know bear hunting season will start this weekend in New Jersey at Bear Mountain-Harriman State Park. I finally talked a few of the guys into moving to a higher level of the game. Everything's been worked out and we're meeting in New Jersey on Friday evening. I won't be gone long; I should be back Sunday afternoon, at the latest."

"That's fine. As long as I don't have to get up before dawn again. Besides, I know how much this means to you and how long you've waiting to hang out with your boys. Enjoy yourself … just make sure you come back home to me."

Robert reached across the table and grabbed hold of Pearl's

hand. "Don't worry about me, don't I always come back, in one piece."

"This time is different ... bear hunting!?"

"I'll be fine."

Pearl had always supported Robert's hobby. She thought, "why not?" At least her man didn't have a hobby of hanging out all night in clubs or strip joints.

Pearl reached across the table and grabbed Robert's other hand. "I love you and you better watch your back. I don't want have to come to Jersey and hurt some bears for messing with my man." Robert flashed a modest grin. He was happy that she didn't ask a lot of questions. His thoughts of Sasha were becoming more frequent. He knew he had to see her, especially after he almost called Pearl Sasha last night. The woman had him hooked, and he had decided not to resist her anymore.

Sasha's phone rang. She glanced down at it and realized it was Robert. She let it ring a few more times, something she did when men she hadn't slept with called. "Hello."

"Hey, it's all set. I'm free to meet you in New York City on Thursday."

"Sounds good. I've made reservations at the Waldorf Hotel in Manhattan. I'll see you Thursday." Sasha hangs up the phone, and starts chanting "Go Sasha, Go Sasha, Go Sasha ..."

～～

Sasha packed nothing but dresses, bullets and motion lotion. She had only one objective this weekend, and that was to rock Robert's world! Sasha got such a pleasure turning a pussy cat into a lion. She wanted to leave Robert craving her.

They both decided to catch different flights. Robert flew into Newark, rented a car and drove to Parsippany, New Jersey to check into the Sheraton Hotel. When he arrived in his room, he started having second thoughts. His nerves were getting the best of him, so he called home. "Hello, honey, how are you?"

"Sweetie, I'm missing you. How was your flight?"

"It was good. What are your plans for the weekend?"

"Oh, I'll probably hang out with Nikki. We'll probably do dinner and a movie. Sweetie, please be careful."

"Don't worry about me, I'll be fine. You just have a good time with Nikki. Tell her I said, Hello."

"Okay, baby … I love you."

"I love you too." Robert placed the phone in its cradle.

"Damn," Robert thought, what am I'm I doing here?

Robert picks up the phone to call Sasha, to tell her he couldn't go through with it. "Hello."

"It's me, Robert."

"Well, hello, you. I was just running me some warm bathwater."

"I'm sorry to interrupt … should I …"

"No, you're fine. It's about 5:00 p.m. I've ordered a car service to pick you up around 6:30 p.m., and I'll meet you at Tao. The driver will know the location, but just in case, it's located at 5th Avenue and 59th Street. With traffic, it's about an hour ride from where you're located. Oh yeah, be sure to bring an overnight bag. I'm looking forward to seeing you."

The only thing Robert could say was, "okay."

Robert arrived at the restaurant a little after seven. He was still nervous about being with Sasha. That quickly ended when the door opened and Sasha turned around and walked over to greet him.

"You are so beautiful, especially, without your work clothes."

Sasha flashed a smile. "Well, thank you, you don't look bad yourself. I hope you're hungry."

The hostess showed Sasha and Robert to their table. Sasha could tell that Robert was a little nervous, so she made sure she kept the conversation alive and ordered Champagne right away. After a few drinks, Robert started to loosen up. That's when Sasha removed her right shoe and slid her naked toes up and down Robert's inner left leg. Robert jumped because he was caught off guard. Sasha didn't care. She kept on moving closer and closer until she found Tarzan. There he was about eight or nine inches and not even erect. Robert began to close his legs but Sasha grabbed one of his hands and started caressing it ... as if to say, *"don't worry, everything is going to be okay."*

"So, Sasha, how was your meal?"

"It was good. I can't wait until dessert, and I have the perfect place in mind to have it."

Sasha paid the tab and they caught a cab to Ray's Champagne Bar. Sasha loved New York, probably because it's the one city that you could be whoever you wanted to be without the fear of being judged by others.

At Ray's, the patrons could care less if they walked inside a couple's cozy private cubby finding lady's panties on top of her mate's head, her dress raised to a very discrete level, and she riding her man in slow, but circular motion as they moved to the beat of the music. The patrons would politely say something like, "my bad," close the curtains, and continue their search for a vacancy.

Of course this was one of Sasha's favorite spots in New York. All of the male bartenders knew her on a first name basis. As you walked down a few steps, you would be entering a dark, but classy looking bar, with private cubby holes. Sasha called in advance to reserve the cubby hole in the far corner with the velvet hot red drapes. R&B music played softly in the background. The waiter had placed the Champagne and fresh fruit she had requested inside their private little paradise. Robert couldn't believe his eyes. As he sat comfortably on the silk and velvet covered pillows, Sasha sat across his lap and started feeding Robert some of the fruit and he sucked each one of her well-manicured fingers after each bite.

"Sasha, hold on ..."

Sasha pretended she couldn't speak nor hear his moans of discomfort. She stood right before him, placing his head on her stomach as she stroked his head. She closed his legs together and placed both her legs around his waist. She moved her waist in a circular motion. Tarzan was tossing and turning determined to find Jane. Sasha reached between their legs to find his zipper. It was time for the two to meet. Sasha reached in her bra, pulled out a condom, and placed it on Tarzan. Jane didn't need any help putting out this fire, she was toooooo wet! It got so good to Sasha, she rested both her arms on the table, and arched back. Robert had to rise just a little so that Tarzan and Jane would not separate. After a half hour of mind-numbing sex, Robert exploded with passion.

"Good Morning." Robert felt more comfortable than he thought he would.

"Good Morning, you're up already? What have you been up to this early?" Sasha had made her way to the bathroom, making sure that she looked presentable.

"I got up around 7:00 a.m. and went downstairs to work out, grabbed some coffee and read the paper. You were resting so peacefully, I didn't want to disturb you. I enjoyed last night.

"You should have, I used some of my better moves on you." Sasha grinned as she leaned in for her good morning kiss.

"So, what do we have planned for the day?"

"I have taken care of everything. You mentioned that you wanted to catch up with a few of your hunting friends, so I've built in time in our schedule for you to do that. While you're mingling with the boys, I could do a little shopping and meet you back at my hotel around six. Then we will do dinner. We have reservations at the Sharke Bar, in Harlem. Afterwards, I'm going to take you to another one of my favorite spots."

"How was hunting with your friends?"

"We had a good time catching up. We spent most of the time at John's Tavern talking about old times." Robert moved closer to Sasha and grabbed her around the waist, pulling her close enough to let her know he wanted her. "How was your shopping?"

"Great! I even got something for you." Sasha was hoping that her feelings weren't showing. She wanted to keep this casual.

"You shouldn't have, you've already given me so much. How could I repay you?"

Sasha pressed her body closer to Robert. "I can think of thousands of ways."

"Don't you think we should start getting ready to go?"

"Awww, don't worry. We have almost three hours before our dinner reservation. We need to kill some time, anyway. What do you think we should do?"

"I'm open."

"Good, why don't we freshen up a little? I'll run us some bathwater, you open some Champagne and turn on some music."

Even naked, Robert was so fine. His shoulders were broad. His skin was a beautifully chocolate. He didn't have an ounce of fat on his body — skin smooth.

Sasha placed candles around the tub and removed her robe. Robert was such a gentleman; he held her hand, as she walked up the three steps into the large and deep circle tub. Before they sat down in the tub, she pulled him close to her, kissing him so deeply she was lost in her thought. Robert's hands began moving all over her body. He caressed her breasts with his hands and tongue. Sasha responded by stroking Tarzan and smearing some motion lotion around his head. She kneeled down in the bathtub, placed her mouth around Tarzan's entire head and sucked off the warm strawberry taste. Robert was so aroused, he sat down in the tub and placed Sasha on top of him at first, but placed both hands around her waist, raised her slowly from the water and pulled Jane to his face. Sasha rubbed some motion lotion on her fingers and Jane and Robert followed with his tongue. Sasha couldn't hold it any longer; her body stiffened and shook as she let out cries of passion. Robert didn't move, he swallowed all of her juices, like a good little boy.

Sasha was so wiped out she could hardly move. Robert lifted her out of the tub and carried her to the bed. He placed her on her stomach, entering her from behind. Sasha was not in control, for once. Their bodies were moving with perfect rhythm. Sasha tried to hold back, but her body wasn't in control now. She began shaking and moaning, trying not to be so loud, but she couldn't stop herself. She came again.

"Whose is it?" Robert asked in a sex-filled voice.

"It's yours! It's yours!" She cried out as he picked her up and guided her across the room. Robert's body was covered in sweat as he lifted Sasha up on the countertop.

"You are the best … best lover …" Sasha couldn't speak as Robert entered her again. Her body was trembling all over. Robert's mouth kissed all the right places on her neck and breasts as he moved in and out of her.

"Don't stop, please don't stop!" Robert continued until they both were satisfied, each collapsing on the floor in front of the fireplace, unable to make it to bed. Sasha had met her match. The mild-mAnered Robert had definitely turned into the King of the Jungle.

Sasha managed to pull herself into the bed, Robert followed right behind her. She thought, "We're going to miss our dinner reservations." She lifted her head to see what time it was. It was 8:45 p.m.. Sasha decided it would just be better to go to bed. They had already been feed enough. A few minutes later, they both drifted off to sleep.

CHAPTER SIX

More
Disappointment
But With Pleasure

MOMMY, HOW DO I look?"

"Baby you are the bomb! You look so handsome in your Tux."

"Mommy, am I going to have to stand up with you in front of a lot of people like last time?"

"Not if you don't want to. Mommy is just glad you are accompanying me."

"Mommy, what does "accompanying" means?"

"That means to go with someone to an event ... like you're going to the awards banquet with me."

"Mommy, is daddy going?

"No, baby. Daddy has something important to do. You'll see Daddy tomorrow. Tee Tee Pearl is going with us to keep you company. Now, push the door bell and let's see if your Tee Tee is ready to go."

Nikki had always given back to her community. For years, she has volunteered for the United Way of the Mid-South and this was her second time receiving an "Outstanding Service Award."

"Eweee, look at Tee Tee's baby, how handsome."

"Thanks, Tee Tee."

"I'm ready, just let me get my purse and I'll meet you guys in the car."

"Okay."

"Hey, are you all right? I see your boy has canceled on you again. So, what was his excuse this time? It couldn't be work, he's not working. It can't be something about his apartment, he lives with you now. So, what is it?"

"He says he helping a friend move his household items from one house to another, and it had to get done by tomorrow. Pearl, he means well. He's just going through a lot right now. I'm sure when he gets back on his feet, things will change."

"You're too good for him! He's taking you for granted. Things will change, but not for your better. Mark my words! It's just my gut feeling."

"Let's get off him. I accepted Matthew's offer for dinner."

Pearl put her hand over her mouth, and started to say something but stop. She started clapping her hands and laughing. "Now that's what I'm talking bout! When and where? What are you going to wear?"

"Will you calm down! I don't want Isaiah to hear. It's tomorrow night, he's taking me to Chez Philippe at the Peabody, and I will be wearing a very nice conservative business suit."

"A suit! Hell no, you need to wear that little red dress with the V-cut in the back."

"Girl, you are too much!"

"Nikki, you look stunning! Red's your color," Nikki is beautiful inside and out. She's 5'5", about 130 pounds, with a caramel skin complexion and wears her hair in a short conservative style. Nikki's make-up was always flawless and her taste for clothing was upscale.

"Thank you, Matt. You look quite handsome yourself."

"Our table is roight over here. I ordered Champagne. I 'ope that's okoy with you." Nikki and Matt get to their table and Matt pulls Nikki's chair out for her. Nikki got a wind of Matt's cologne. She just loved that Polo Black fragrance. Before she knew it, she said, "I just love the way that Polo Black smells on you."

"Thanks awfully, Nikki."

"I didn't mean to be so blunt."

"Nikki, we're not working. So relax ... roight?"

"Yes, but, it's hard to relax around you. You make me very nervous."

"Don't mean to." Matt rested his hand on top of one of Nikki's hands and said, with his sexy accent, "Oi really want you to feel comfortable 'round me."

Matt poured Champagne into both their glasses and proposed a toast. "'Ere's to the start of summat special." Their glasses slightly touched. Nikki couldn't seem to control her heart from beating so fast. She was trying to figure out why she was so excited.

"So, Nikki, tell me 'bout yourself ... sommat personal."

"Well, I have a son named Isaiah who I cherish. He's takes very good care of me."

"I can see that. He's doing a bang-on job of it. Tell us more."

"Well, let's see. I spend most of my free time with my son, but I enjoy working out, spending quality time with my siblings and plotting my future. At the end of my day, I meditate and ask God for strength to do it all over again."

"Oi knew you were special. Oi'm so 'appy you took me up on me many offers." Matt smiled.

"Matt, I must tell you that I'm still involved ..."

"Nikki, oi don't mean to interrupt, but oi'd be a fool to think you weren't taken. It's only supper. Let's enjoy this moment. But to make meself clear, as long as you're single, oi'm going to be aftah you, because oi believe you were placed on this Earth for me."

A tear fell from Nikki's eye. These were words she longed to hear from Brandon. Matt leaned over to wipe the tear gently from Nikki's eye and placed a kiss tenderly on her cheek. In the heat of passion, Nikki turned her head, closed her eyes and met Matt's lips. They kissed.

"Excuse me, sir, are you ready to order?"

Chapter Seven

New Beginnings

*P*EARL THOUGHT SHE WAS dreaming when she opened her eyes and felt Robert's tongue moving in a circular motion around her clit. She looked over at the clock; it showed that it was 7:00 in the morning. What is Robert doing under this comforter? Pearl lifted up the comforter, "What are you doing?"

"I thought you said you wanted some morning sex." Robert laid on top of Pearl, his body touching hers made her wet. "Do you still want me?"

Pearl wanted to say, *"Hell yeah, I want you. I've wanted you to do this for years! What took you so damn long?"* She decided to nod her head and let Robert do what he wanted to do. Thoughts starting running through her head, "What was it? Was it her new perfume? Her new thong underwear with the matching tank?" Robert disappeared under the comforter again, he quieted all of her thoughts when she felt his tongue glide over her clit. Her body began to quiver. She was so wet she didn't know what to do next.

Robert rolled over and pulled Pearl on top of him. She hadn't been on top in so long she almost forgot how to ride. Robert guided her every step of the way. Pearl let out a loud cry as her small framed hips moved up and down.

An hour later she lay on her husband's muscular chest

wanting to say so many things, ask so many questions, but she couldn't find the words.

"I love you Pearl."

A tear fell from her eye.

"I know you do."

They fell into a peaceful slumber.

For some reason, Brandon couldn't snap out of the daze he was in. Since his father's death nothing seems to be working right. Moving in with Nikki hasn't made things better. To let Nikki tell it he never even tried to look for a "real job," or at least a comparable position to the one he had at United Package. Material things didn't seem so important these days for Brandon. He was tired of living off Nikki. Brandon made a promise to himself that his moving in with Nikki would be temporary. He refused to let others think that he was being kept by his baby's momma.

Nikki was so happy Brandon moved in with her and Isaiah. It had been eight years since they had become a couple. It's time, Nikki thought, they would finally become a family, officially. Nikki tried not to put too much pressure on Brandon, because of all he'd gone through the past year. So she put aside her needs and started focusing on the fact that Isaiah needed his father.

Nikki gently placed soft kisses on Brandon's soft lips. "Good Morning, Baby. How did you sleep?"

"Okay I guess."

"Do you think you could pick Isaiah up from Karate practice around 3:00 p.m.?"

"No, I've made other plans."

"Other plans? …okay, so when do you plan to spend some

quality time with your son? This is the third time I've asked you to help me out with Isaiah and you always have something else planned.

"Please don't start Nikki. I'm not your houseboy. Everyday you have some kind of errand for me to run. How did this get done before I moved in?"

Nikki took a deep breath, silently counting to herself so she wouldn't explode. "You know Brandon, I've tried to work with you. I have put aside my need for attention from you, but I can't keep putting off the attention that your son needs. What is so important that you can't pick your child up from his class?"

"I'm going to cover Tyrone's shift at the Center. I need the extra money."

"Why, it's not like I ask you for anything."

Brandon yanked the black silk sheets off him, quickly got out of bed, and closed the bathroom door behind him. He thought, 'why does she always have to remind me that she's paid, that she doesn't need a damn thing from me or anyone for that matter.' Brandon paced back and forth in the bathroom, talking to himself. "Why am I here? Nikki doesn't need a man, she needs a butler. Besides, I hate picking up Isaiah from Karate school, especially since I didn't help pay for the classes."

Nikki was passed the point of being sad, she was pissed off. Tears start to well up in her eyes, but she refused to cry. "Not today girl, you will not cry over this man today. He's the one that's wrong not you. No more tears about him."

Nikki started getting ready for work. She called Pearl. "Hey girl."

"Hey what's up?" Pearl sounded tired.

"Will you be able to pick Isaiah up from Karate today? Brandon refuses to do it."

Pearl could hear the irritation in Nikki's voice. "Is every-thing okay?"

"It will be. I don't mean to cut you short, but I have a meet-ing, can you pick him up?"

"Yes. I will be happy to see my little man today."

"Thanks." Nikki hung up the phone and continued get-ting ready. She ignored Brandon the rest of the morning, even when he tried to kiss her goodbye.

~~

"Adam, you're going to be late for your swimming lessons if you don't get a move on!"

"Okay Momma, I'm trying to find my goggles."

"Look in inside your chest, left side compartment."

"I found them, mom, you're the greatest!"

"Yeah, Yeah, you just hurry yourself down here so you can eat and we can go. You're going to have to eat this pop tart in the car. Let me hold it until you put on your seat belt."

"Mom, are you ever going to have a boyfriend?"

Star raised her eyebrow, trying to catch a glance of Adam's face in the rearview mirror. "Where is this coming from? Why do you ask?"

"I just want you to be happy. Malik's mom got a boyfriend and she smiles all the time now. I want you to smile more."

"Well, I'm happy that you're thinking about my well-being, but I'm okay. Anyway, there's no one that interests me right now."

"How about the guys at the Center? They look like they like you."

"What do you mean by that?"

"It's just that I see the other mothers drop off their kids and the guys don't run to hold the door open for them, or ask them how they are doing, like they do for you."

Star was a 5'1", 35-year-old Latino who looked every bit of twenty-five. She made it a point to hide her natural beauty. She had a humble spirit, wore her hair in a ponytail most of the time and preferred dressing very casual. Star hadn't dated anyone seriously since her husband passed away nearly six years ago. It was a little flattering for Star to hear from her son that she had some secret admirers.

"Would you be upset if mommy had a boyfriend?"

"No, I see other mommies with their husbands; I don't want you to be alone."

"Baby, I'll never be alone … I have you." Star parked the SUV, and walked her son to the front entrance of the Center. And like clock work, the security guard on duty rushed to open the door, and asked Star how was she. Star smiled and simply responded, "I'm well and you?"

"I'm better now."

"See, mommy I told you! Adam laughed as he ran off with the other boys to prepare for his swim lessons.

"Can I get in on the inside joke?" Brandon smiled as he moved a little closer to Star. He had been looking at her for a while now. He just wasn't sure how to approach a woman that seemed so sweet, innocent and pure.

"Oh, it's nothing. It's really nothing."

"You have such a smart and disciplined son. I guess I should not only be giving you credit for that, I'm sure his father deserves a little credit as well."

"Adam's father passed away several years ago. He really didn't get a chance to know him."

"I'm sorry to hear that. I just lost my father about a year ago. You have done an outstanding job with Adam."

"Thank you so much. I must admit he is wise beyond his years."

Brandon felt like a teenager again. He couldn't stop smiling. "I know Adam loves swimming. I know the Swim Coach for the University of Memphis. Would you and Adam like to go to a college swim competition?"

Star didn't mean to flirt, but she found herself touching Brandon's shoulder. It was easy to talk to him. She had always been attractive to Black men. "Adam would love that! Let me talk it over with him, and let you know."

"That sounds good to me. Don't keep me waiting too long.

Here's my cell number. Call me anytime."

"Okay. I'll let you know." Star grinned and made her way back to her car, careful not to turn around and look at him. It had been years since she had enjoyed the attention of a man, and she didn't want to seem desperate.

Brandon pushed back his feelings of guilt. He knew that he should be ending things with Nikki, but he had been with her for so long. Things just weren't going to work out.

Brandon first noticed Star about a week after he started working full-time at the Center. She was the opposite of Nikki. She wasn't high maintenance, from what he could see, Star lived a simple life. She was a school teacher. She was not a flashy dresser, didn't wear a lot of make-up, and drove a very conservative SUV. Whereas, Nikki had to have designer this and designer that. She had to go to the day spa at least once a week for either a facial, massage, manicure or pedicure. She drove a two-seater convertible gold interior and exterior Jag in the summer and spring months and a Range Rover in the fall and winter months. Star seemed very easy to talk to and be around.

CHAPTER EIGHT

Hooked

Sasha hadn't heard from Robert in three days and decided to send him a text message to shake up his day.

Robert was in a Team meeting when he received Sasha's text message. It read, "Jane is in distress and needs Tarzan bad."

Robert always got excited by Sasha's direct and aggressive behavior. He had never met anyone like her. She would say and do just about anything. He loved the attention.

"Robert what do you think?"

"Oh, oh, I'm sorry can you repeat the question?"

"The new tower will be twice as high as the current one. It will go from 110ft tall to 225ft from ground to cab floor. How long do you think it would take to install the sensor technology to aviation and airport security? I was under the impression that you have done some research in this area?"

"The installation will take around a year, assuming we start within the next sixty days."

"Well, that's it for today."

Robert couldn't wait to get back to his office and call Sasha on her private telephone line.

She answered on the third ring. "I got your message."

"You did. How is your day going?"

"Better now."

"Oh yeah, and why is that?

"Because, you always seem to know how to brighten my day. You are something else."

"Yes, I am. So, would you like to hook up this weekend? I have a buddy pass you could use. I was thinking about Atlanta, this time. Are you game?"

"I'm game."

"Okay, since I'm only giving you a few days notice. Let's say we fly down to the ATL on Saturday afternoon. I have listed you tentatively on the 3:00 that would get you there around 4:00. I will arrive early afternoon. White Glove Limo Services will meet you in the baggage claim area. We'll stay in the Penthouse Suite of the Ritz Carlton Hotel, Downtown. Ask for Niya and she will direct you to me."

Robert didn't even try to hold back his smile. He thought about Sasha all the time, even the morning he made love to Pearl. "I'm there. See you Saturday."

"Jane will be waiting."

~·~

Brandon finally got the call he had been waiting for. Unfortunately, he was having dinner with Nikki when the phone rang. He looked down and seen Star's name flashing across the screen.

"I'm sorry Nikki I have to take this." Brandon went into the bathroom so he could talk in private.

He picked up his phone, careful not to speak to loudly. "Hello."

"Hello, Brandon?"

"Yes."

"It's me, Star. I hope I didn't catch you at a bad time."

"No, no I was hoping you would call."

Star tried not to smile, but she was happy that he wanted to hear from her. "Well, Adam has been jumping up and down ever since I told him about the swim meet. Is it okay if we still go?"

"Of course it's okay. I will pick you up around 3:30 on Saturday. Will that work for you?"

"That's perfect; I will call you later this week with directions to my place."

"See you Saturday." Brandon hangs up the phone and makes his way toward the door. He stops for a moment, not wanting to seem too happy. He thought that would be unfair to Nikki, since they hadn't been getting along, lately.

Things were starting to improve for Brandon. Nikki helped him get an interview with FedEx, and he just got the news that he would be starting in a week. He was too excited about taking Star and her son to the swim meet at the University of Memphis. It was something about Star that made him felt at ease. He feels no pressure at all.

CHAPTER NINE

BROKEN PROMISES

Nɪᴋᴋɪ ᴡᴀs sɪᴛᴛɪɴɢ ᴀᴛ the kitchen table when Brandon came in. Her eyes were red and puffy. She didn't let Brandon take off his uniform before she started questioning him. "I found these apartment finder books on your dresser. Were you going to bother telling me you were moving out?"

"Yes, but, you knew from the start that my living here was temporary. And now that I've gotten this job at FedEx, I don't need to continue to live off you."

"Forgive me, but I thought we were working towards becoming a family. Did I miss something?"

"Nikki, you just can't expect me to live by your schedule. Because you want to get married and settle down, I'm supposed to be ready. When you were in law school, and started working for that damn firm, settling down was not even on your mind. But now since you're ready, I'm supposed to just drop what I'm doing and fall in your line?"

"You know that's not my intention. I thought you felt the same as I do, but I clearly see you do not. You know I'm not going to beg you to stay, if you want to move out, that's fine with me. It's Saturday and I need to go to the office for a few hours to catch up on some work. Can you keep Isaiah?"

"I've made other plans this morning. If you take him to Pearl's house, I will pick him up later this afternoon."

"How do you know Pearl's is available to watch Isaiah? Isaiah is your son, not Pearl's."

"Mom, is everything all right?" Isaiah came out of nowhere, forcing Nikki to calm down. The last thing she wanted was for her baby to see her upset.

"Yes, baby. Why don't you go back into your room and let me and daddy talk for a moment."

"You know what Nikki, I'm late, and I have to be going. We need to pick this conversation up later."

Brandon moves toward Isaiah and kneels down so he can look him in the eyes. "Hey son, I'm going to pick you up later this afternoon. We can go to Jillian's and do some bowling. Does that sound like fun?" Isaiah nods his head yes.

"Goodbye Nik I will call you later."

～・～

"It's one o'clock, are you guys ready?"

"Yes, we're ready and Adam is too hyped!"

"Hello, Mr. Brandon! Thanks for taking us to the swim meet."

"You're welcome, Adam."

"Mom, can we go to Applebee's after the swim meet?"

"I don't know son, we can't just impose on Mr. Brandon's time. He may have other plans."

"No, I'm available. We can go."

Brandon could not believe he had just agreed to Adam's proposal. He knew that he was supposed to pick up Isaiah this afternoon. Brandon wanted to spend as much time as possible with Star. After all, she didn't know his history or current situation. He enjoyed the feeling of Star looking up to him, counting on him. Star made him feel like the man Nikki wanted him to be. Being around Star was effortless for Brandon. He was drawn to her grace.

CHAPTER TEN

LET THE TRANSFORMATION BEGIN

*O*HHH, DON'T STOP, OHHH right there, yes, yes, yes, that's it, that's it. Oh you're fucking me right!

Sasha and Robert move deeper and deeper into each other. Robert moans letting Sasha know she is doing her job right.

"Damn this bathroom is just too small." Sasha pulls away. "Just a second, let me turn around, and then we can get back to business." Sasha turns around; Robert smacks Sasha on her ass until she moans with pleasure. He pushes himself inside of her as deep as he can and resumes making her have the multiple orgasms she has grown accustomed to.

Club Kit Kat, in the ATL, was another one of Sasha's and Robert's reading spots. When you entered this club, it's dark, red crushed velvet all around the walls on the first level. As you walked down stairs you could hear the wild sounds of house music. On your immediate left there was a bed. Now, you won't see just anybody pouncing around on "the bed," only the big ballers! There's a $500 dollar minimum drink tab before you could even rest your bottom on top of the bed and enjoy all the pleasures that this club gadget has to offer! So, that's level two. As you went down a few more steps, you enter "The Dungeon," where you saw all types of private spots for a twosome, threesome, whatever gave pleasure. Then there was the most popular spot of all, "The Bathroom." It was equipped with all kinds of free sexual gadgets (condoms, whipped cream, motion lotion, bullets, vibrators, edible undies, anal balls, penis rings, etc). You could take all the time you needed, just kindly tip security on your way out. This was just one of many of Sasha and Robert's sexual excursions, not to mention the numerous times they had had sex in Sasha's office.

The next morning on their way to the airport, guilt started to sink in Robert's mind. He was not only feeling guilty, but he was just plain old tired. He had been trying out these sex lessons from Sasha on Pearl. It had become overwhelming trying to satisfy two wild women.

As they waited for their stand-by flight, Robert confessed, "Sasha, you are such a beautiful woman and you deserve so much better than these sexual escapades. I never thought I had some of the feelings that you have helped me discover. You have given me something that I will always cherish. You have made me feel good about living and I have a new perspective on life. You have such a free spirit and I feel myself out of control at times. I hope we can continue to be friends, but I can't continue this. The guilt is tearing me apart. I must make things right with myself and my life at home with my wife. I'm sorry."

Sasha was careful not to show how disappointed she was. She had heard this speech a few times before, and she knew Robert couldn't offer her anything but sex. Sasha knew from the start not to let her emotions get in involved.

So, Sasha replied with a soft smile, "Don't be sorry, I understand. It was fun while it lasted." She rubbed Robert's hand and turned her attention back to her Essence magazine.

"*That's it!*" Robert thought. He anticipated the discussion to go another way. Robert didn't understand … he knew Sasha was into him. He started thinking about last night, how their bodies and minds mutually met and became bonded, somehow. She had to feel something, that kind of connection can't be faked. How could she just be okay with what he had just said? Shouldn't she be upset or at least disappointed? Was she even human?

~~

Brandon's phone started to ring as he was moving his stuff out of Nikki's place. He knew it was Star; they were talking three or four times a day. He loved to hear her voice. He had even worked up the courage to tell her about Nikki. She felt uncomfortable, but she understood and trusted that Brandon would handle the situation with care.

"Hey, it's me. I was calling to see if you wouldn't mind escorting me to a banquet this Wednesday night?"

"I would love to. What's the occasion?"

"I've been nominated for the "Teacher of the Year Award". It's not a big deal, if you rather not, I would understand."

"I'm honored that you even ask me. What time should I pick you up?

"How about 6:45? The dinner starts at 7:30."

"It's a date! See you then."

Star hung up the phone and wondered how in the world his ex-girlfriend let him go. Brandon was everything she'd been longing for and needing in a man. He treated her son like his own; he was supportive, secure of himself, and not to mention he was fine-as-hell. She had to look up to the Lord and thank him at least three times for bringing Brandon into her life.

CHAPTER ELEVEN

There's Good Change & Bad Change

Nikki came home to find all of Brandon's clothes and personal items gone. It felt so empty without his stuff there. She knew she couldn't pretend any longer, it wasn't good for him, her, and especially Isaiah.

She sat on the edge of her bed remembering the conversation she had with him earlier that morning. He was so peaceful and kind about the whole thing.

"Nik, we need to talk. I found an apartment and I'm moving out. I will pick up my things later this afternoon. I want to thank you for everything you've done for me. I'm not ready or able to give you what you need and deserve. You're such a beautiful woman with so much love to give. You deserve someone who knows how to appreciate and love you as much as you love them. I'm not that person. I'm sorry. I do love you and I hope one day you will find in your heart to forgive me."

Nikki was speechless. She always knew deep in her heart that Brandon didn't love her as much as she loved him. She thought she could love enough for the both of them until he realized how much he really did love her. She cried for all the years she had wasted, for all the promises he had made to her, and for her son. She was the most hurt by all of this, but none of that seemed to matter to Brandon. This was about him being the man. Nikki was forced to admit that she couldn't make him love her.

~·~

Pearl knew that the day would come when Robert would finally satisfy her intimate desires the way she always dreamed. She thought to herself all of the expensive sexual treats she purchased from Victoria's Secret have worked a miracle on Robert. He was more romantic and attentive to her sexual needs, regardless of the time of day. She knew she could whip him into shape one day … she just had to be patient.

~·~

After six months of working 10-12 hour days and sometime weekends, Brandon was promoted to a Senior Manager at FedEx. Somehow, the more time he spent with Star and Adam the more focused he became on getting his life in order. He purchased a home and began to spend more time with Isaiah.

Brandon even tried to build a friendship with Nikki, but Nikki didn't want anything to do with him, especially after she had found out about Star. Nikki had been on a few dates with Matt, but she couldn't bring herself to be with anyone else. Brandon had her heart, and it was painful to see him happier without her.

Chapter Twelve

Your Work in Action!

One Year Later

ROBERT WAS STANDING AT the counter ordering his coffee when he caught a glimpse of Sasha, still looking fabulous, out of the corner of his eye.

"Can I help you sir?" The clerk from behind the cash register asked.

"Oh, I'm sorry. I would like a regular coffee, grande please."

Robert turned quickly to see where Sasha was, to his satisfaction she was right next to him. Seeing her still gave him goose bumps.

"Sasha, hello. How are you? Haven't seen you in awhile."

Sasha flashes her perfect smile, fighting away flashbacks of the last time she felt him inside of her. "I'm doing fine. I got a new position that requires me to travel a bit more. I'm actually on my way to London. What have you been up to?"

"Sasha, do you have time to sit and talk? I've wanted to talk to you."

"Sure."

"Sasha, I must start off by saying you look great!"

"Thank you. You don't look so bad yourself. Matter of fact, you look different, in a good way. I really can't put my finger on it."

"Sasha, my life has changed in so many ways and I have

you to thank."

"What do you mean?"

"I can't believe I'm even sharing this with you. But, you've always made me feel as though I could talk to you about anything. I never knew life could be so fulfilling. I've been focusing a little less on work and a lot more on enjoying life. Being with you showed me that there is a lot of pleasure in life. Pearl is expecting, and I couldn't be happier."

Sasha thought in a sarcastic way, another satisfied customer ... yippy for me!

"Congratulations to you and Pearl. What else can I say? I aim to please."

Houston's is one of Pearl and Nikki's favorite places to dine. As Pearl and Nikki follow the hostess to their window-view booth, Pearl glances across the room and thought she recognized Brandon sitting with some plain-Jane looking woman.

Pearl leans over the table, careful not to bump her expanding stomach. "Nikki, is that who I think it is?"

"Yes, it is, but why is he on his knee? Did he loose something?"

"No, it looks like he found something, his nerves. Can you believe that shit? He's proposing to her!"

Brandon caught the attention of most of the patrons sitting near him. When he opened the tiny, black box there sat something very shiny. Couldn't tell if it were a carat or more. Brandon stopped speaking and placed the shiny object on Star's ring finger. She opened her arms as wide as she could, and shouted, "Yes, yes, yes!" The patrons begin to congratulate the newly, engaged couple by applauding.

Nikki got up from her seat and Pearl, very dignified shouted, "Nikki, where are you going? Hold up, hold up." Nikki walked towards Brandon's table as if she were mesmerized. When Brandon saw Nikki coming his way, his smile immediately transformed to a nervous grin.

"Congratulations, Brandon."

"Nikki, hello. Hummn, thank you."

"So, aren't you going to introduce me to your fiancé?"

"Yes, this is Star. Star this is Nikki, Isaiah's mother."

Nikki wanted to smack him, it had been just over a year and he was ready to marry this woman. She couldn't believe what she was seeing. Nikki extended her hand to Star. "It is good to finally meet you. May I?"

Star nods her head, proud to show Nikki the ring that Brandon had just put on her finger.

Nikki raises Star's left hand to get a closer look at her engagement ring and says, "Brandon, you have very good taste. I wish you both all the best." Nikki lowers Star's hand and politely turns and walks away. For some reason, unbeknownst to Nikki, she couldn't cry or even get upset for that matter. She felt relieved or closure. She instantly felt her spirit telling her everything is going to be all right.

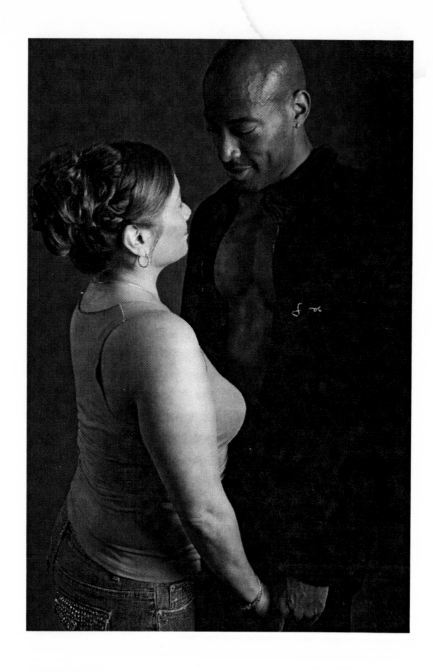

EPILOGUE

FOOD FOR THOUGHT

*F*OR ALL OF THE Nikkis out there, there's nothing you can do to change an insecure man. An insecure man is out of any real woman's league. Don't get sucked into his good loving and his every-now-in-then, charm. Save yourself some years of heartache and let him go! You're only molding him for the next woman.

∽∾

Now, for all of you Stars out there in the world, you must give credit where credit is due and recognize the "Ex-Girlfriends" for prepping these brothas, for you. Stop making comments like, "how did she let this good man slip away?" You weren't a party to their relationship. You've only heard his side of the story! Keep in mind that he didn't obtain all of his present talent alone. If it weren't for ex-girlfriends, sisters, mothers, or some other woman in his past, he wouldn't be the man he is today.

∽∾

Some women have the power to influence men to do whatever, whenever, others do not. Pearls, if your man has only made love to you at a certain time of day and location for a number of years, and then all of a sudden he's "Mr. Spontaneous," this should make anybody say, "huummmm." I'm not saying don't reap the benefits from his extra-marital affairs, I'm just saying don't try to take all the credit!

~~

If it weren't for the Sashas of the world, some marriages would just die of boredom.

~~

Brandons, how much longer is it going to take for you to understand that a real woman needs more than just material things? We do believe in our hearts you have so much more to offer; however, it's up to you to find it, accept it, embrace it and demonstrate it, consistently! So, put aside your insecurities and love us. It's that simple. And when you do decide to love us, be sure to keep this verse in mind:

> *Love is patient, love is kind. It does not envy, it does not boast, it is not proud. It is not rude, it is not self-seeking, it is not easily angered it keeps no record of wrongs, love does not delight in evil but rejoices with the truth. It always protects, always trusts, always hopes, always persevere. Love never fails. I Corinthians 13:1-8.*

~~

Ladies, I'm just keeping it real. If he's not reciprocating his love for you, simply, let him go. You're too good for him! The more time you spend grooming him, some other woman will reap the benefits of your work. Be strong, and remember, don't put all of your love and trust in man. True love can only be experienced one way, and that is through the Father. He is the only Man that will never let you down.

~·~

I hope you enjoyed getting to know these sistahs
and learning how they spent their time
grooming this fine brotha — just for you.

NOTES

Notes

NOTES

NOTES

NOTES

Printed in the United States
66506LVS00003B/202-285